The Mystery of
Magillicuddy's Gold

This book belongs to:

Warrior _____

will, God's Mighty Warrior™
series includes:

Will, God's Mighty Warrior™
The Mystery of Magillicuddy's Gold

And just for girls:
gigi, God's Little Princess™
series includes:

Gigi, God's Little Princess™
(in book and DVD formats)
The Royal Tea Party
The Perfect Christmas Gift
The Pink Ballerina

will

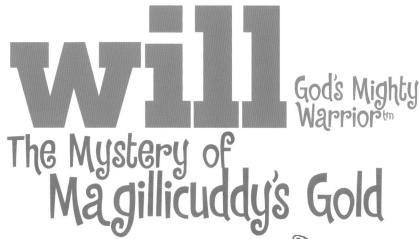

God's Mighty Warrior™

The Mystery of Magillicuddy's Gold

By Sheila Walsh

Illustrated by Meredith Johnson

Tommy NELSON®

A Division of Thomas Nelson Publishers
Since 1798

www.thomasnelson.com

WILL, GOD'S MIGHTY WARRIOR™: THE MYSTERY OF MAGILLICUDDY'S GOLD

Text © 2007 by Sheila Walsh

Illustrations © 2007 by Tommy Nelson®, a Division of Thomas Nelson, Inc.

All rights reserved. No portion of this book may be reproduced in any form without the written permission of the publisher, with the exception of brief excerpts in reviews.

Will, God's Mighty Warrior™ is the trademark of Sheila Walsh, Inc. Used by permission. All rights reserved.

Published in Nashville, Tennessee, by Tommy Nelson®, a Division of Thomas Nelson, Inc.

Tommy Nelson® books may be purchased in bulk for educational, business, fundraising, or sales promotional use. For information, please e-mail SpecialMarkets@ThomasNelson.com.

Scripture quoted from the *Holy Bible, International Children's Bible*®, copyright © 1986, 1988, 1999 by Tommy Nelson®, a Division of Thomas Nelson, Inc.

Library of Congress Cataloging-in-Publication Data

Walsh, Sheila, 1956–

   The mystery of Magillicuddy's gold / by Sheila Walsh ; illustrated by Meredith Johnson.

     p. cm. — (Will, God's mighty warrior)

   Summary: Will finds a piece of a treasure map in a bin of used books, and when he goes back to search for the rest of the map, the bookstore owner shows him that the real treasure in life is found within the Bible.

  ISBN 13: 978-1-4003-1028-9 (hardback : alk. paper)

  ISBN 10: 1-4003-1028-8

  [1. Christian life—Fiction. 2. Pirates—Fiction.]   I. Johnson, Meredith, ill. II. Title.

PZ7.W16894My 2007

[E]—dc22

                     2006029398

Printed in China

07 08 09 10 11 LEO 5 4 3 2 1

This book
is dedicated to the
spirit of adventure
deep within the
heart of every
little boy.

"Avast there, Ralph the Great!" Will called
out to his dog. "I fear the seas are turning
nasty! Batten down the hatches, Josh,"
Will shouted to his first mate. "We're
headed for a bumpy ride!"

"Aye, aye, Captain," Josh replied.

Will and Josh had very busy lives. On any given day, they might be hunters or astronauts or Chinese acrobats, but today they were pirates.

"Where shall we put our prisoner, Captain?" asked Josh.

"Throw her in the brig!" Will answered. Lola seemed quite happy to be a prisoner.

"Ralph the Great, do not let the prisoner out of your sight!"

Ralph the Great took his job very seriously and plopped down in front of the cardboard-box brig.

"There will be no pulling of the Captain of the Guard's tail, either!" Josh warned prisoner Lola. "Any trouble from ye, and we will make ye walk the plank!"

Lola was thrilled at the prospect.

"Land ho!" Will shouted as he saw his mother bringing lunch.

"Ahoy, mate!" he called. "Will ye help me tie up me ship?"

"Aye, Captain, I will help ye!" Will's mother answered with a smile as she caught the garden hose Will tossed in her direction. "What's Lola doing in the brig?" she asked.

"She's our prisoner," Josh said. "We captured her just off the coast of Madagascar as the sun was rising."

"Well, I'm afraid your prisoner needs her lunch and a nap," Will's mother replied, carrying a reluctant Lola to freedom.

"What's our plan now, Captain?" Josh asked.

"'Tis the search for Magillicuddy's Gold!" Will said.

"Arr!" Josh agreed. "Where be the treasure map?"

Will looked around to make sure there were no spies before he produced the map.

He whispered the words on the map:

To Samuel Magillicuddy,
May your life be forever changed by the treasure within.

"Me thinks part of the map is missing," Josh said. "Who is Pirate Magillicuddy, and where is this treasure?"

"Aye, that is a mystery, and I have a secret tale to tell ye, Josh!" Captain Will replied, leaning over to whisper in his friend's ear.

That night after Will said his prayers, he decided to tell his father about the secret map too. "Dad, can we go back to the bookstore where I got my pirate books?" he asked.

"Sure, we can do that," his father replied. "Is there something special you're looking for?" Will put his finger to his lips as he checked outside the bedroom door for spies. . . .

Lowering his voice to a whisper, Will answered his dad, "I'm looking for the rest of the treasure map to Magillicuddy's Gold. Part of it was stuck to the back of one of the pirate books I bought with my allowance."

"A treasure map!" Will's dad said. "May I see the map?"

Will reached under his pillow and retrieved the mysterious document.

"Hmm, it looks a little like the first page of a book," his dad said.

"We have to get the rest of the map," Will said. "It must be somewhere in the store! Will you take Josh and me?"

"We'll go on Saturday. But for now, it's off to sleep, young pirate. Sweet dreams and quiet seas!"

The following Saturday, Will and Josh waited impatiently on the front doorstep until Will's dad appeared.

"Shall we fly our flag out the window?" Will asked, brandishing his favorite pirate flag.

"Well, you might want to stay undercover until we get there," his father suggested.

"Good plan, Dad!" Will said.

As soon as Will's dad parked the car, he and the two young pirates headed for the bookstore.

"Look at the name above the door," Dad said.

Will and Josh looked up and saw:

Magillicuddy's Treasure House of Books

"A pirate's disguise if ever I've seen one," Will said.
Josh agreed.

They entered the store on high alert.

Will looked to the right and to the left—and when the coast seemed clear, he whispered to Josh, "Over there!"

In the corner of the store was a large chest marked: Used Books—$1.

"Is that where you found the book that the map was stuck to?"
Josh asked.

"It is," Will answered, barely able to keep his voice under control.
"The rest of the map has to be in that chest."

"Can I be of any assistance?" a friendly voice asked.
Will and Josh turned around and stood toe-to-toe with . . .

"I'm Mr. Magillicuddy."

The boys swallowed hard. Could this be the pirate himself?

"No, sir," said Will. "Thank you, but we are just fine, just totally fine and could not be more fine—if we were any finer, we would be far too fine!"

Mr. Magillicuddy laughed. "Just let me know if I can be of any help to two such fine young pirates."

"That was a close one, Will," Josh said.

"Too close," Will agreed. "Now, let's find the rest of the map."

The boys dug into the chest through all kinds of books. They dug deeper and deeper, all the way to the bottom, but there was no map.

"Any success, boys?" Will's dad asked.

"No, Dad, we can't find it," Will said. "That Pirate Magillicuddy must have suspected I was on to him after our last trip."

"May I see the part of the map that you have?" Will's dad asked.

Will pulled the map from inside his shirt.

"Be careful, Dad. Be very careful."

Will's father approached Mr. Magillicuddy. "Excuse me, sir.
I wonder if you recognize this?" he asked. Will and Josh gasped.
They couldn't believe what Will's dad had done.

"Indeed I do," Mr. Magillicuddy replied. "I've been looking for
that. It must have dropped from my book when I was turning
the lights off one evening. I am so glad you found it."

"All is lost!" Will cried.

"No, no, young man," Mr. Magillicuddy said. "All is not lost—quite the reverse. What this book tells us is that all is found!" The boys looked at each other in total disbelief.

Mr. Magillicuddy put the CLOSED sign on the door. Then he invited his guests into a tiny sitting room in the back of his store, where he served them homemade lemonade and explained the mystery.

"When I was about your age, I wanted to travel on great adventures. Then my father lost his job, and it was a hard blow for all of us. I didn't think I'd ever have an adventure, much less find a treasure, and then—"

"You became a pirate!" Will said matter-of-factly.

"No, no," Mr. Magillicuddy said, laughing. "That's when I was given the book."

"And it had a treasure map in it?" Josh asked.

"Well, in a way," Mr. Magillicuddy replied. "I was given a Bible."

"You mean there's treasure in the Bible?" Will said.

"More than any pirate's chest in the whole wide world could ever hold," Mr. Magillicuddy answered.

"Excuse me, I'll be right back." Mr. Magillicuddy stood and left the room. When he returned, he had two books. "I have something for you two young pirates," he announced, "a treasure of your very own."

That afternoon, Will and Josh sat outside near their ship.

"Look what my Bible has written in it, Josh!"

Josh leaned over and read out loud from Will's Bible,
"'To Will: May your life be forever changed by the treasure
within.' Look, Will! Mine has the same thing, only it starts
'To Josh.'"

"Josh, listen to this:

Even boys become tired and need to rest.
Even young men trip and fall. But the people who
trust the Lord will become strong again. They will
be able to rise up as an eagle in the sky.
                                        —Isaiah 40:30–31

 Josh, being a pirate is nothing. . . . I think God might want
us to fly!"

Try with all
your heart to gain
understanding. . . .
Hunt for it like hidden
treasure. . . . then you
will begin to know God.
Proverbs 2:2,4,5